THIS BOOK
BELONGS TO

_____

_____

A LITTLE OWL BOOK

The Little Match Girl

retold by Glynis Langley
illustrated by David Fryer

WORLD & WHITMAN

The story of The Little Match Girl was written by Hans Christian Andersen, a Danish writer of the nineteenth century, who is thought by many people to be the greatest writer of children's stories ever to have lived. The sad and moving story of The Little Match Girl is a perfect example of his work.

It was bitterly cold that New Year's Eve, and snow was beginning to fall in the town. Occasionally a carriage would go racing by, taking its occupants to some fine and sumptuous festive celebration, but few people had ventured out on foot.

A poor little girl was wandering about those dark, cold streets. She was bareheaded and barefoot. She had been wearing slippers when she left her home, but they were much too big for her, having once belonged to her mother. And, anyway, she had lost them now.

Her slippers had fallen off her feet when she ran across the road to avoid two carriages rolling by. One of them was not to be found anywhere in the road, and the other had been stolen by a wicked boy, who ran off with it before the little girl could stop him.

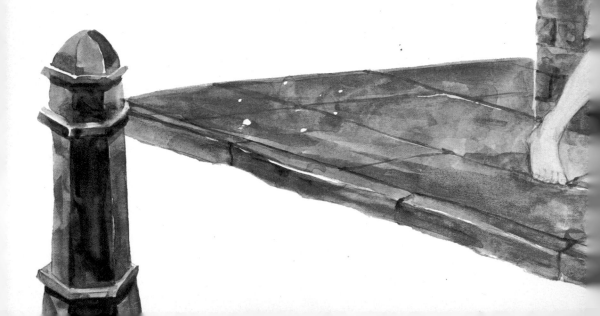

The poor little girl walked on, and by now her hands and feet were blue with the cold. Her clothes were ragged and torn, and she wore an old apron, in the pocket of which she carried her bundle of matches, all apart from half a dozen, which she held in her hand.

Her matches were for sale, but nobody had bought any that day. She was hungry and miserable. The snowflakes settled on her pretty yellow hair, and she knew that she would have to look for some shelter.

Lights were shining from the windows of the fine houses, and there was a wafting smell of roast goose everywhere, for this was the traditional fare on New Year's Eve in that town. What a delicious smell it was!

The little girl found a corner where one house projected a little further than the next, and here she crouched, trying to curl herself into a tight ball for warmth. She dared not go home, for she had not sold a single match, and her father would be angry.

And besides, it was not much warmer in their attic room. The wind whistled through cracks in the roof, no matter how hard they tried to stuff them up with rags and straw. No, she wouldn't go home . . . she might as well stay in her cold little corner.

If only she dared light just one match. . . . Yes, that's what she would do, to warm her hands a little! She struck a match on the wall. *Scritch!* It spluttered and blazed into flame, burning like a candle with a bright, clear flame.

And what could she see in the flame? Why, it was extraordinary! She fancied that she could see herself, sitting in front of a big stove with polished brass feet and handles. A fire was blazing in the stove, and it seemed to her that she could just stretch out her feet and warm herself by it. . . .

But no! The match went out, the warm stove disappeared, and all was cold and darkness again. She struck another match, and as the light blazed up it fell upon the wall of the house where she was sheltering. And where the light fell the wall seemed to become like glass, and she could see right through to the room inside.

What a wonderful sight it was! The table was laid for a fine festive meal, with pretty crockery, and shining glasses, and gleaming silverware. Best of all though, was the large roast goose which was about to be carved. And as she watched - could it be true? – that same roast goose stood up, waddled off the table, and walked towards her!

Then that match went out too, and the scene disappeared from view. The Little Match Girl struck another match. This time she could see herself sitting beneath a beautiful Christmas tree, lit from top to bottom by thousands of candles. The little girl stretched out her hands towards the tree . . . then out went the match again.

This time it seemed as though all those Christmas candles were rising higher and higher, until she could see that they were really the twinkling stars of the sky above.

Suddenly one of the stars fell from the sky, making a bright streak of light across the darkness above.

"Now someone is dying," thought the little girl, as she watched the falling star. Her old grandmother, the only person who had ever been really kind to her, had told her long ago that whenever a star falls it means that a soul is going up to God.

The Little Match Girl watched the star and remembered her grandmother's words. She struck another match against the wall, and this time – yes! – it was her grandmother who appeared in the circle of flame. The little girl could see her quite clearly, and she looked so gentle and happy as she smiled down at her grandchild.

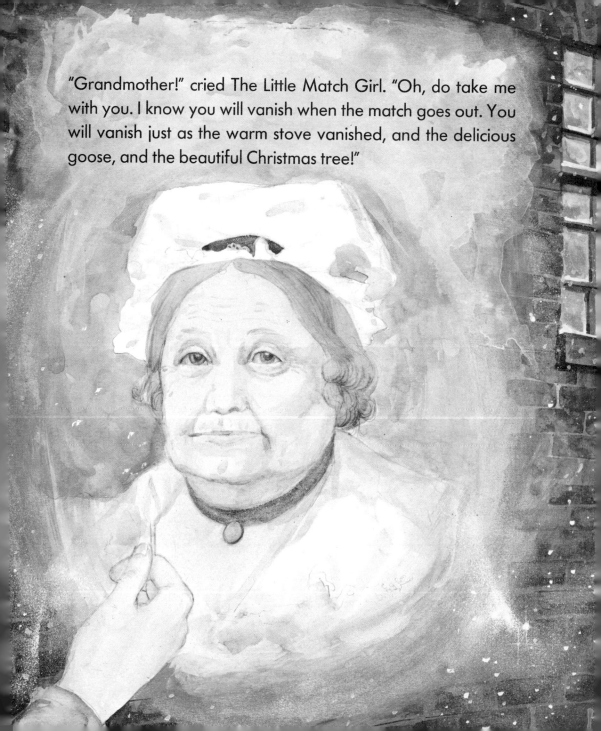

"Grandmother!" cried The Little Match Girl. "Oh, do take me with you. I know you will vanish when the match goes out. You will vanish just as the warm stove vanished, and the delicious goose, and the beautiful Christmas tree!"

She began to strike her whole bundle of matches, quickly, one after the other, because she longed now to keep her grandmother beside her. The light of the matches lit up the cold corner as bright as day, and her grandmother had never before looked so good or so beautiful.

She lifted The Little Match Girl up into her arms, and together they soared up in a halo of light and joy. Up, up, they flew, far above the earth, to a place where there was no more cold, no hunger, and no sadness. For now they were with God.

In the cold morning light the people of the town found The Little Match Girl sitting in the corner between the houses, with pale cheeks and a smile on her face. She had frozen to death on the last night of the old year.

Now it was New Year's Day, and they gathered round the poor little girl, whom no one had even noticed in the cold streets of the night before. She was sitting with the spent ends of her bundle of matches still in her lap.

"She must have tried to warm herself with her matches," they said. "Poor thing." But none of them knew what wonderful visions The Little Match Girl had seen that night. And none of them knew that she had gone with her beloved grandmother to a place which is greater than all places, in that glorious halo of light.